# Contents

# To the Teacher

The activities in this manual have been developed to prepare students to engage both academically and personally in their reading. The activities may be used in part or whole.

The Model Lesson Plan prepares students for understanding and appreciating the plot of the novel. The additional activities enable students to develop their own responses. The Cooperative Learning Activities challenge students to understand the point of view of each character, as well as the complexity of each character's motivations and decisions. The Activity Sheets and quizzes allow you to assess students' understanding of what they have read.

## Teaching the Classics

Teachers of literature know that a study of the classics, the body of literature that has a recognized position in literary history for its superior qualities, is a necessary ingredient of a comprehensive language arts program. Defining the term *classics* does not go far enough in exposing students to what those superior qualities are. To gain an appreciation of the classics, students need to be given a sense of the authors' purposes for creating the works, while being encouraged to apply their personal insights to the stories. This overview suggests ways of presenting the classics that will help your students understand why the classics have survived through the years and why, even today, they continue to be relevant and appealing to readers everywhere.

First, ask your students to explain what they consider to be the important qualities of a good story. Are believable, realistic characterizations important? Are appealing themes important? Should the writer's style be remarkable in any way? In discussing these elements, ask students to give examples of literary works or authors who have demonstrated these qualities.

Discussion of the suggested questions presents an excellent opportunity to acquaint students with some of the important elements of a novel:

**Character**—If a story is to live, the people in it must be real. What makes characters real? How do we learn about people we're meeting for the first time? What things do we notice about them? What do these things tell us? During the novel, do any of the main characters change? How? Why do these changes happen? Are these changes believable? Students reading *The Grapes of Wrath* may determine a great deal about each of the major characters from the first scenes in which they appear. Students may be able to see how each character's subsequent actions can be predicted by the way he or she is portrayed in the beginning.

**Theme**—Ask students to determine the main idea of the novel and to express it in their own words. How is this idea expressed in the novel? In words? In action? In consequences of action? Have students select passages or events in the novel that support their opinion of what the novel's theme is. Is this idea still important today? How would a person of today understand the theme of *The Grapes of Wrath* differently from the way a person of the 1930s would?

**Plot**—Studying how an author organizes the events in a work can help students appreciate literary classics. Often, an author gives clues about the actions of the characters. Students reading *The Grapes of Wrath* should look for these clues as the action unfolds. By looking for clues during their reading, students can improve their understanding of the story.

**Setting**—Why is knowing the time and place of a novel important? Do the things people say and do change when the story takes place long ago? Why? What is the setting of *The Grapes of Wrath*? Have students distinguish between the general setting (the Great Plains and California in the 1930s) and the setting of a specific scene (a migrant workers' camp). Ask students to consider whether this story could take place today. What seems unique to the time and place?

**Style**—What do we mean by a writer's style? How does style affect the mood of a novel? Are there things that might happen in a serious novel that would not happen in a humorous one? What is the style of *The Grapes of Wrath*? What is the overall feeling? What scenes, moments, or action convey the novel's mood? What scenes, moments, or action are in contrast to this mood?

**Tone**—Ask students what mood the author has tried to create through description, images, and dialogue. Is it suspenseful? Sad? Serious? Have them find descriptions or dialogue to support their answers.

# Model Lesson Plan

## Activity:
## The Importance of Character Development

## Objectives

1. To understand the characters in *The Grapes of Wrath*.
2. To understand how the author makes the characters seem real.

## Introduction

Tell the students that they will create a plot chart before they begin to read *The Grapes of Wrath*. They will add to it as they read the novel. Explain that the purpose of the chart is to help students understand how events in the plot affect the characters.

## Motivation

1. Ask students what they already know about the Great Depression of the 1930s. Keep track of their prior knowledge by listing the points they make on the chalkboard. If students have no prior knowledge about the Depression, allow some time for research on this topic. Schedule a class session in the library, or provide research materials in your classroom and have students browse through them.
2. Have students make a chart like the following

one. Ask them to fill out the boxes under the "You" column by writing how *they* would feel if they experienced the events listed in the "Events" column. Tell them that they will continue to fill out the chart as they read.

| Character Reaction in *The Grapes of Wrath* | | | | |
|---|---|---|---|---|
| Events | Ma | Pa | Tom | You |
| Loss of Home | | | | |
| Loss of Work | | | | |
| Long Trip by Car | | | | |
| Job as Fruit Picker | | | | |
| Unfair Employer | | | | |
| Flooding | | | | |

3. After students have filled out the top row of boxes, have them meet in groups of four to share their ideas. See "Cooperative Learning Activities" on page 12.
4. As students read the novel, have them fill in the chart by indicating how Ma, Pa, and Tom react to each of the events listed.
5. You may wish to have students meet again

after they have filled out the entire chart for a post-reading discussion on the characters and how Steinbeck makes them "real" by having them react to situations in realistic ways. You may wish to have students look at their charts and determine which character they can best relate to.

## Additional Activities

1.  Before students begin to read the novel, invite them to look at the cover illustration and to flip through the book, looking at the interior illustrations. To stimulate interest, you might wish to elicit comments from the students about their favorite pieces of art. Ask them to speculate about what is happening in each picture.
2.  Have students write a journal entry that one of the characters might have written about any of the events in the novel.
3.  Suggest that students make a time line that highlights the main events in *The Grapes of Wrath*.
4.  Have students write two separate lists. The first is a list of reasons the Joads might have had for leaving Oklahoma. The second is a list of reasons they might have had for going back.
5.  Give students about 20 strips of paper, and have them write a simple sentence on each one. Each sentence should describe one thing that happens in the novel. Then, students can exchange sentence strips with partners and organize the strips in the proper order.

# Reproducible Masters

These activities are designed to assess students' progress during and after the reading of the novel. Included are a Mid-Book quiz, an End-of-Reading quiz, and an Activity Sheet that includes a cause-and-effect exercise. These reproducible masters allow the teacher to check students' basic understanding of the novel's plot, themes, and character development. Answer Keys for the Reproducible Masters can be found on page 18 of this Teacher's Manual.

Name _____    Date _____

# Activity Sheet
## CAUSE AND EFFECT

**B.** The chart below lists several events that occur in the story. In some places, the *cause* of the action or event has been given. In other places, the *effect* is listed. Fill in the blank spaces. You may look back at the book if you need help. The first one has been done for you.

| CAUSE | EFFECT |
|---|---|
| Tom is released from prison early for good behavior. | He arrives home in time to go to California with his family. |
| 1. | The family cannot afford a nice funeral for Granma. |
| Tom trips a deputy who is trying to arrest an innocent man. | 2. |

| Ma | | | | | |
|---|---|---|---|---|---|
| Pa | | | | | |
| **Rose of Sharon** | | | | | |

## B. FILL IN THE BLANK
Choose an answer from the box to fill in the blank.

> living in a boxcar with another family, the Wainwrights
> taking the blame for Tom's tripping the deputy
> not able to find enough work in the area
> avoiding the flooding
> suspected of leading a strike
> helping the poor folks fight back

1. The reason the family decides to leave the government camp is that they are

   _____

2. The reason Jim Casy goes to jail is that he is

   _____

3. While in jail, Jim Casy discovers that his true calling is

   _____

4. Granma doesn't get to see California because she
   a. loses her eyesight along the way
   b. decides to stay with Noah
   c. dies before the family gets there
   d. goes back to Oklahoma.

5. One thing Connie Rivers does in the book is to
   a. study radios
   b. study tractors
   c. study to become President of the United States
   d. leave Rosasharn.

6. The Farmers' Association doesn't like the government camps because
   a. the people get too used to good treatment
   b. they think the camps mistreat the people
   c. they have too many dances
   d. the camps occupy too much good farmland.

**3.** Pa thinks that the reason Noah is strange is that Pa was responsible for accidentally

_____.

**4.** Muley Graves helps the family at the last minute by

_____.

**5.** To get to California, the Joads set off

_____.

**6.** Ma is worried when Tom crosses the state line because it means that he is

_____.

## C. MATCHING

Match the quotation to the character who said it. Write the character's name on the line. Choose from these characters: Tom Joad, Ma, Jim Casy, Granma, Pa, Muley

**a.** brother and sister      **b.** cousins

**c.** best friends      **d.** husband and wife

## B. FILL IN THE BLANK

Choose a phrase from the box to fill in the blank.

> chopping cotton and selling some of their things
> agreeing to take two of their dogs
> breaking the terms of his parole
> killing a man in self-defense
> hurting him when he was being born
> traveling down Highway 66

1. The reason Tom Joad had been in prison was that he was convicted of

   _____

   _____.

2. The Joads get money for their trip out west by

   _____

   _____.

Name _____    Date _____

# Mid-Book Quiz

## A. MULTIPLE CHOICE
Circle the letter of the correct answer.

1. Where is Tom Joad going when the story opens?
   **a.** to jail   **b.** home   **c.** California   **d.** an unnamed state

2. In which state does the story open?
   **a.** Oklahoma   **b.** Arizona   **c.** Texas   **d.** California

3. What had Pa Joad been doing for a living?
   **a.** He was a farmer.   **b.** He was a preacher.
   **c.** He was a teacher.   **d.** He was a fisherman.

4. What is the cause of Grampa's death?
   **a.** starvation   **b.** pneumonia   **c.** stroke   **d.** heart attack

5. What weather conditions cause trouble for the Joads in Oklahoma?
   **a.** snow and sleet   **b.** hurricanes and rain
   drought and dust storms   tornadoes and thunderstorms

2. "Maybe all men got one big soul that everybody's a part of."

3. "Ma, there's a couple of fellows just come along the road. They wonder if we could spare a bite."

4. "Preacher? You got a preacher? Go get him. We'll have a grace."

5. "I'd like to have a couple of dogs. I'll take 'em."

6. "What we got left in the world? Nothing but us. And now, right off, you want to bust up the folks—"

# End-of-Reading Quiz

## A. MULTIPLE CHOICE
Circle the letter of the correct answer.

1. Some people on their way back to Texas tell the Joads that they will soon be called
   a. bums
   b. vagrants
   c. thieves
   d. Okies.

2. What does Noah decide to do?
   a. stay at the river
   b. get a job to help the family
   c. get married
   d. go back to Oklahoma.

3. The reason the Wilsons stay behind at the river is that
   a. they want to do some fishing
   b. Sairy is dying

**5.** While they are picking cotton, the Joads are

_____

**6.** The reason the family moves to higher ground is because they are

_____

_____

## C. SHORT ESSAY

Choose one of the questions below. Answer it by writing one paragraph on a separate sheet of paper. Use evidence from the novel to support your answer.

**1.** How does Jim Casy have an effect on Tom Joad's life?

**2.** What is the most important thing to Ma?

**3.** If Tom Joad were a real person, would you like to have him as a friend? Why or why not?

# Activity Sheet

## CHARACTER DETAILS

**A.** As you read the novel, complete the chart with details you learn about each character. Look at this chart to help you think about the actions each character takes and why.

### MAIN ACTIONS OF CHARACTERS

| Name | Chapters 1-2 | Chapters 3-4 | Chapters 5-6 | Chapters 7-8 | Chapters 9-10 |
|---|---|---|---|---|---|
| Tom Joad | • hitches a ride home<br>• talks to truck driver | | | | |
| Jim Casy | | • tells Tom he "lost the call"<br>• asks to go | | | |

| | |
|---|---|
| **4.** | Tom hits a man in the head with an ax handle. |
| **5.** | Tom has to leave the family. |
| Al falls in love with Aggie Wainwright. | **6.** |
| **7.** | Rose of Sharon loses her baby. |
| Heavy rains cause the stream near the boxcars to overflow. | **8.** |

# Cooperative Learning

Included in this manual are three Cooperative Learning activities. These activities are included because cooperative learning has been shown to have great value.

Cooperative Learning activities are structured so that students work together in small heterogeneous groups. Effective groups, or teams, reflect the mix of students in a classroom.

Cooperative classroom activities not only depend on group or team formation, but also require that students depend on one another in a positive way. Activities are structured so that if one student does a good job, all the students benefit. Teachers have reported that the performance of the entire team improves if the team's success is based on each individual's success. Team members know that they will let the team down if they do not perform well.

Social skills are developed as a result of students working together in cooperative groups. Students learn that to reach common goals, they need to listen to one another, resolve conflicts, set and revise procedures, keep on task, and encourage others. Careful planning and a clear explanation about the structure of activities are necessary to ensure success.

The positive effects that cooperative learning has on students include: 1) more time on task, 2) greater role-taking abilities, 3) improved student relations, 4) better academic performance, and 5) a more positive attitude.

# Cooperative Learning Activities

## Activity 1
## Conversational Discussion Groups

After students have prepared their character charts, they will be ready to share their ideas. The discussion groups do not have to limit their conversation to the charts. Group members can raise any book-related questions they want to talk about. They may also use the "Thinking It Over" questions at the end of the book to stimulate ideas.

The purpose of Conversational Discussion Groups is to create an atmosphere in which readers can discuss a book and share ideas.

To ensure successful Discussion Groups, follow these steps:

1. Set up heterogeneous groups of six to eight students to work together.
2. Review/introduce the rules.
   (Take turns. Stay on the subject. Ask for clarification when you don't understand something. Let everyone talk.)
3. Have a copy of the book for each student.
4. Monitor discussions from a distance.
5. Conclude by asking questions such as:
   - How did you go about getting answers today?
   - How did that method work?
   - How would you change your way of working next time?

# Activity 2
# Interviewing a Character

Students should complete this activity after they have read the book. The activity requires students to assume two roles, interviewer and interviewee. The interviewee can be any of the major characters in the novel.

1. **One-Way Interview**
   Ask each student to assume the role of one of the characters in the novel. Divide the class into teams of four. Each team is broken into two pairs. In each pair, one student is the interviewer, and the other is the interviewee. The interviewee will answer questions in the role of the character they have chosen. The interviewer may ask questions as themselves, or may conduct the interview in the role of the character they have chosen. The interviewer will ask questions about the interviewee's thoughts and feelings concerning the various things that happened in the novel.
2. **Reverse Roles**
   In this step, students switch roles, with the interviewer becoming the interviewee and vice versa.
3. **Round Robin**
   In this step, each student, in turn, shares some of the things he or she learned during the interview with the other three team members.

## Variation for Groups of Three
For groups of three, at Steps One and Two, two team members interview the third member.

# Activity 3
# Presenting a Scene

Have cooperative groups collaborate to prepare a performance of a scene from the novel. Make sure that groups are not duplicating scenes. Suggest that the groups choose scenes where there is a role for everyone, whether it is an off-stage role as a support person or a role as an actor.

Group members can divide the jobs of props person, sound-effects person, and actors. Allow each group sufficient time to rehearse, and have them present their scene to the class.

If the scenes are particularly well done, arrange for students to present the scenes to another class, and then discuss the importance of the novel with the other class.

# Answer Key

## REVIEWING YOUR READING

### Chapter 1
**1.** D  **2.** C  **3.** D  **4.** A  **5.** B

*Thinking It Over*
**6.** The evidence in this chapter that family relationships were important is found in the fact that the women and children knew they were safe as long as their men "were whole."

### Chapter 2
**1.** A  **2.** C  **3.** D  **4.** B  **5.** C  **6.** A

*Thinking It Over*
**7.** Answers will vary. Tom might be warmly welcomed because the family is close. He might not be welcomed because times are so tough that one more mouth to feed could make things even more difficult for the family.

### Chapter 3
**1.** C  **2.** D  **3.** A  **4.** B

*Thinking It Over*
**5.** Answers will vary. Steinbeck included sections that are independent of the Joad family saga. Students should be able to see that these sections provide background information and present universal themes.

### Chapter 4
**1.** A  **2.** C  **3.** A  **4.** A

## Thinking It Over
5.  Ma Joad is generous, even though she is poor.
    She is willing to share what little food the
    family has with strangers. She is strong and
    loving. Her warm welcome of Tom shows how
    much she loves him.

## Chapter 5
1. A  2. D  3. A  4. B

### Thinking It Over
5.  If a grower has twice as many job applicants
    as he needs, he can offer less pay. Perhaps the
    grower offered 40 cents an hour, but 1,000
    people showed up for 200 jobs. The grower can
    then offer only 20 cents. Even if most of the
    people walk off, there will be plenty left who
    are desperate enough to work for almost
    nothing. Evidence can be found on page 43.

## Chapter 6
1. B  2. C  3. D  4. A  5. B

### Thinking It Over
6.  Answers will vary. One explanation for having
    Granma and Grampa die before they get to
    California is to show their connection to their
    home. Once they lost the land in Oklahoma,
    their lives had less meaning to them. Their
    deaths also show how the rest of the Joad
    family now has less of a tie to the past.

## Chapter 7
1. A  2. C  3. D  4. A  5. C  6. C

### Thinking It Over

7. Answers will vary. Connie could stay with Rose of Sharon, abandon her, or leave her temporarily. If he chooses the third option, he could either rejoin her later or send for her.

### Chapter 8

**1.** A  **2.** D  **3.** B  **4.** A  **5.** B

### Thinking It Over

6. Answers will vary. Students will probably realize that the government didn't have enough funds to do so. They might also guess that those who didn't like the migrants could keep more camps from being built.

### Chapter 9

**1.** A  **2.** B  **3.** C  **4.** C  **5.** C  **6.** A

### Thinking It Over

7. Answers will vary. Any President would have had trouble finding an answer. One solution would have been to make it a crime to destroy food while people were hungry. Also, the crops could have been bought by the government and given to the poor, but this would not have solved the housing problems of the poor.

### Chapter 10

**1.** A  **2.** B  **3.** B  **4.** C  **5.** A  **6.** B

### Thinking It Over

7. Answers will vary. It is most likely that Tom will never see his family again, because they have no way to get in touch with Tom later.

# REPRODUCIBLE MASTERS

## Mid-Book Quiz

**A. 1.** b  **2.** a  **3.** a  **4.** c  **5.** c  **6.** d

**B. 1.** killing a man in self-defense  **2.** chopping cotton and selling some of their things  **3.** hurting him when he was being born  **4.** agreeing to take two of their dogs  **5.** traveling down Highway 66  **6.** breaking the terms of his parole

**C. 1.** Tom Joad  **2.** Jim Casy  **3.** Pa  **4.** Granma  **5.** Mulcy Graves  **6.** Ma

## End-of-Reading Quiz

**A. 1.** d  **2.** a  **3.** b  **4.** c  **5.** d  **6.** a

**B. 1.** not able to find enough work in the area  **2.** taking the blame for Tom tripping the deputy  **3.** helping the poor folks fight back  **4.** suspected of leading a strike  **5.** living in a boxcar with another family, the Wainwrights  **6.** avoiding the flooding

**C.** Answers will vary, depending on the question chosen. Check students' answers for support from the novel.

## Activity Sheet

**A.** Answers will vary.

**B.** Answers may vary. Examples include:

**1.** The family spends almost all the money they have to get to California.  **2.** Casy takes the blame for Tom and goes to jail.  **3.** Casy is killed.  **4.** Casy is killed.  **5.** Ruthie tells someone that Tom killed a man.  **6.** Al and Aggie get engaged.  **7.** Rose of Sharon is malnourished because the family does not have enough money for good food.  **8.** The Joad family takes shelter in an abandoned barn.